The Scary Slopes

MY 1ST GRAPHIC NOVEL®

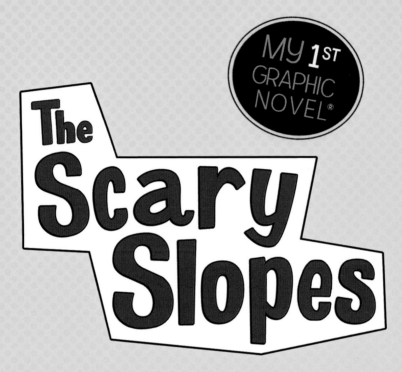

MY FIRST GRAPHIC NOVELS ARE PUBLISHED BY STONE ARCH BOOKS
A CAPSTONE IMPRINT
151 GOOD COUNSEL DRIVE, P.O. BOX 669
MANKATO, MINNESOTA 56002
WWW.CAPSTONEPUB.COM

Library of Congress Cataloging-in-Publication data is available on the
Library of Congress website.

ISBN: 978-1-4342-2534-4 (library binding)
ISBN: 978-1-4342-3062-1 (paperback)

Summary: Brooke and her family are headed to the mountains for vacation. Brooke wants to
snowboard, but she is scared. Her sister, Amy, isn't scared at all. Will Brooke be able to face her
mountain fears?

Art Director: **KAY FRASER**
Graphic Designer: **HILARY WACHOLZ**
Production Specialist: **MICHELLE BIEDSCHEID**

Photo Credits: Shutterstock: Paul Clarke, 4, 5; anse, 18, 14 (bottom); bunadruhu, 6 (top);
Deborah Aronds, 7; Elnur, 14 (top); Gorilla, 22, 23 (top); Greg Kieca, 6 (bottom); Igor Janicek,
11, 14 (bottom), 21; Junne, 16 (bottom); karnizz, 10; leonid_tit, 19; MaxFX, 9; nikolpetr, cover,
16 (top), 17, 25; Ozerov Alexander, 12 (bottom), 13; tungtopgun, 15, 20, 29; Univega, 12 (top)

Printed in the United States of America in Stevens Point, Wisconsin.
092010
005934WZS11

The Scary Slopes

written by **Darcy Pattison**   illustrated by **Steve Harpster**

STONE ARCH BOOKS
a capstone imprint

HOW TO READ
A GRAPHIC NOVEL

Graphic novels are easy to read. Boxes called panels show you how to follow the story. Look at the panels from left to right and top to bottom.

Read the word boxes and word balloons from left to right as well. Don't forget the sound and action words in the pictures.

The pictures and the words work together to tell the whole story.

Amy and Brooke were leaving for vacation.

They couldn't wait to get to the mountains and go snowboarding.

Brooke stared at the snowy peaks. They looked big and scary.

After the long drive, the family stopped at the ski lodge to get equipment.

Brooke and Amy picked out helmets and gloves.
Then they picked out snowboards and boots.

They bought everything they needed to go snowboarding.

The next day, snowboard school started. Brooke put on her gear. She was worried.

The teacher made everything look easy. She went right. She went left.

Amy turned her board down the slope. She was moving but not very fast.

Brooke turned her board down the slope. She was moving but way too fast!

Brooke tried again and again, but she kept falling. What a day!

The next day, Brooke rode on the ski lift with her dad. Amy rode with her mom.

The ski lift climbed to the top. Getting off, Amy did not fall. Brooke did.

Dad asked the ski patrol to take a family picture.

The easy slopes had green signs. Mom, Dad, Amy, and Brooke followed the green signs. Brooke fell and fell.

Mom and Dad had to wait for her while Amy zoomed along.

At lunch, Brooke threw her helmet and gloves.

After lunch, Dad and Amy went to one slope.

Mom and Brooke went to a different slope. Brooke watched how Mom moved her legs and feet.

Finally, Brooke snowboarded down a green slope without falling.

The next day, the weather was great. It was the perfect day for snowboarding.

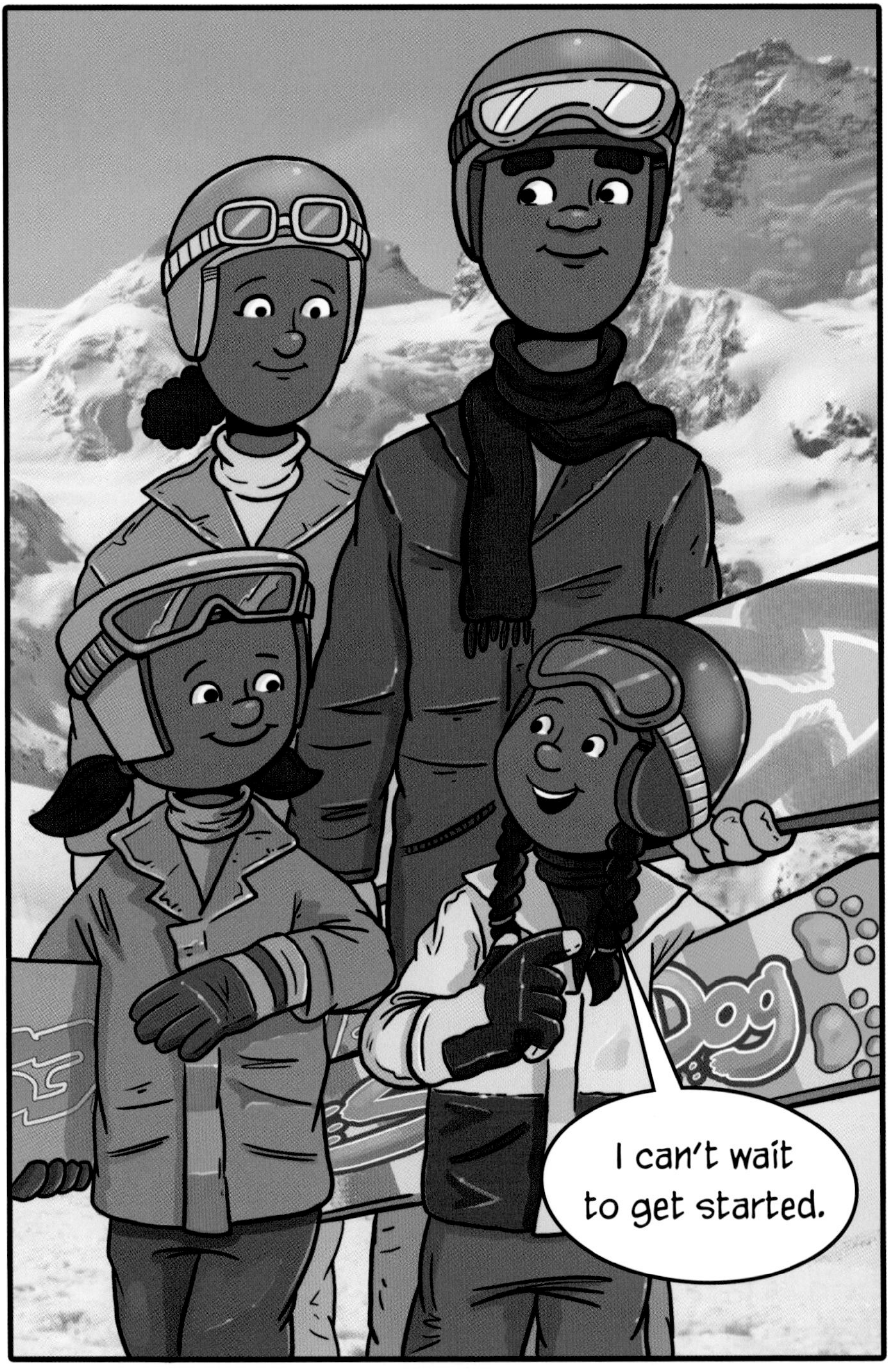
Dog
I can't wait to get started.

The family snowboarded the green slopes.

They tried a harder blue slope. Brooke did not
fall at all!

The last time down the slopes, Brooke and Amy raced.

Amy won, but Brooke was right behind her.

At the end of the day, the family returned all their snowboarding gear.

They picked up the family pictures and packed the car.

Driving home, Brooke looked at the snowy peaks.
They still looked big, but they didn't look scary.
Now, the mountains looked fun.

BIOGRAPHIES

DARCY PATTISON has written nonfiction and fiction for many children's magazines, including *Highlights* and *Clubhouse*. She has a B.A. from the University of Arkansas and an M.A. from Kansas State University. She lives in North Little Rock, Arkansas, with her husband and four children.

STEVE HARPSTER loved drawing funny cartoons, mean monsters, and goofy gadgets since he was able to pick up a pencil. Now he does it for a living. Steve lives in Columbus, Ohio, with his wonderful wife, Karen, and their sheepdog, Doodle.

GLOSSARY

LODGE (LOJ) — a hotel at a ski resort

PEAK (PEEK) — the pointed top of a mountain

SKI PATROL (SKEE puh-TROHL) — skiers whose job is to give first-aid and rescue

SLOPE (SLOHP) — an angle

SNOWBOARD (SNOH-bord) — a board for riding on snow

VACATION (vay-KAY-shuhn) — a fun trip away from home

Brooke's Gear Guide

Snowboarding turned out to be fun, but it was a lot of work. I fell a lot! I was super happy I had the right gear so I didn't get hurt.

First Layer:
1. Fitted Shirt
2. Fitted Pants or Leggings
3. Proper Snowboarding Socks

Second Layer:
1. Fleece Jacket or Sweater
2. Snowboard Pants
3. Snowboard Boots

Third Layer:
1. Hat or Helmet
2. Goggles
3. Snowboard Jacket
4. Gloves
5. Snowboard and Bindings

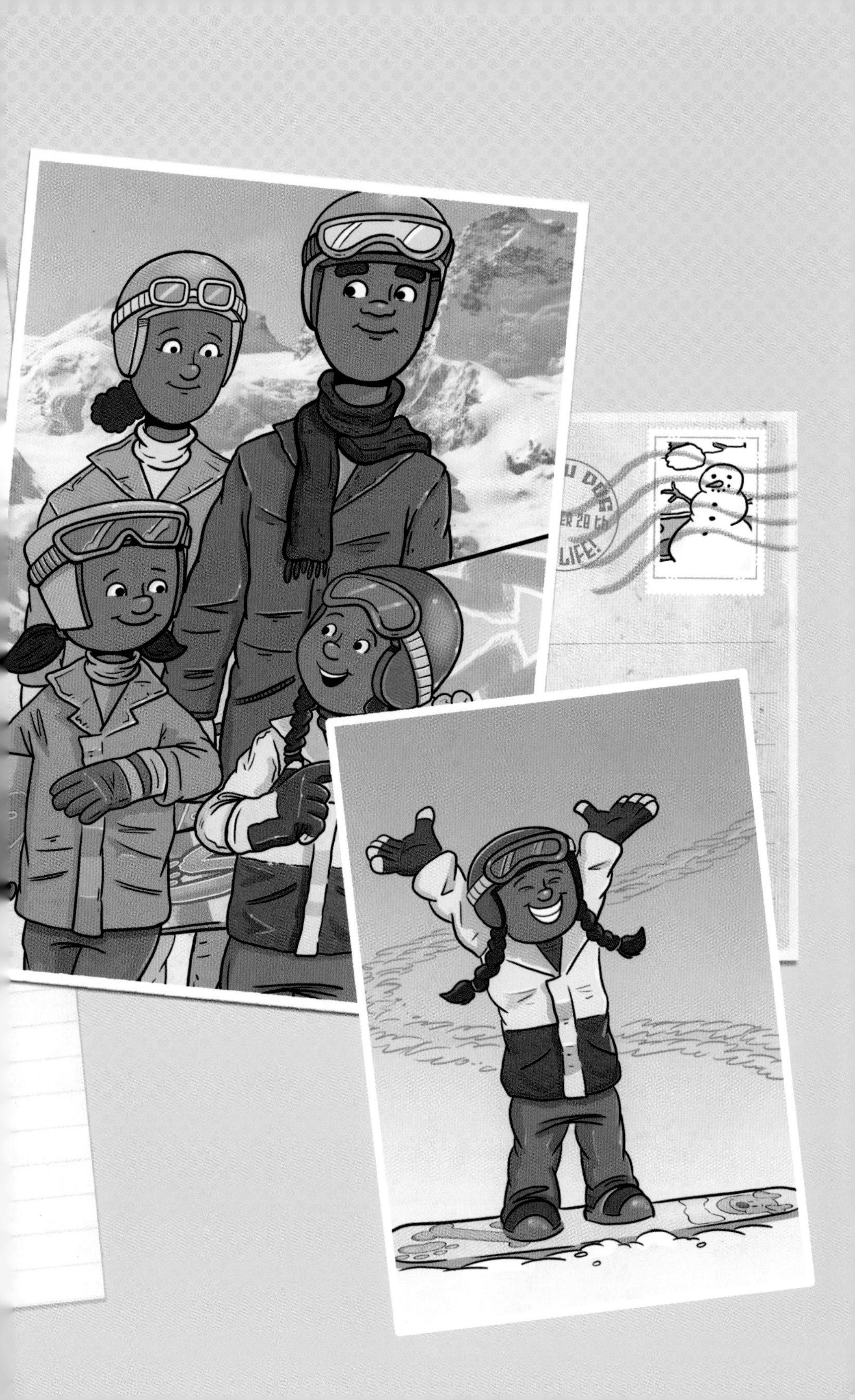

DISCUSSION QUESTIONS

1. Would you like to go to the mountains? Why or why not?

2. Brooke was mad because she could not snowboard easily, but she didn't give up. Tell about a time you didn't give up.

3. Who did you think would win the race between Brooke and Amy? Why?

WRITING PROMPTS

1. Make a list of at least five things you can do in the snow.

2. There are many winter activities. Pick your favorite and write a small paragraph about it.

3. Brooke was scared to try something new. Write a small paragraph about something you're scared to do.